KNIGHT IN TRAINING

TO THE RESCUE!

VIVIAN FRENCH
AND DAVID MELLING

Hodder
Children's
Books

First published in Great Britain in 2017
by Hodder Children's Books

A Catalogue record for this book is available
from the British Library

ISBN 978 1 444 92236 3

Printed and bound in Great Britain by Clays Ltd, St Ives plc

MIX
From responsible sources
FSC® C104740

The paper and board used in this book are made from wood from responsible sources.

Hodder Children's Books
An imprint of Hachette Children's Group
Part of Hodder & Stoughton
Carmelite House
50 Victoria Embankment,
London EC4Y 0DZ
An Hachette UK Company
www.hachette.co.uk

www.vivianfrench.co.uk   www.davidmelling.co.uk

For the wonderful children at Auchinleck Primary,
St Patrick's Primary in Auchinleck, and Ochiltree
Primary, with love.
VF

For Bosiljka
DM

Sam J. Butterbiggins
and Dandy the doodlebird

Prunella

Snapper
and Gibble

Bob and Geoff

Weebles

Dora

THE DARK
DARK FOREST

Dear Diary,

Oops! I'm so excited I can't write properly.
Dandy's tutting at me for being messy, but
I can't help it because today is the most
important day of my life. Today's the day
when I get to do my sixth task, and if I
get it right - TA DA!!!!

I'll be a Very Noble Knight-

CRASH!

The door to Sam's bedroom flew open, and his cousin Prune burst in.

"Sam! What are you DOING?"

Sam put his pen down. "I was just writing my diary—"

"DIARY?" Prune's expression made it very clear that she had no time for such things. "Put it away! We've got to find out what to do next. You've got your horse, and your sword, and your shield, and you've learnt your knightly skills, and" – she puffed out her chest – "you've got the best True Companion a knight-in-

training could ever have.
That's five tasks done –
and only one to do! So
let's get going!"

She grabbed Sam's
arm and began dragging him
towards the doorway. Sam
whistled to the doodlebird,
and the three of them
hurried down the winding
turret stairs.

"Ma and Pa have gone out for the day," Prune said cheerfully. "They're taking the hippogriff home to Lady Hacker. He only arrived yesterday, but he howled all night without stopping. Ma says she can't possibly call it Luxury Holiday Accommodation for Regal Beasts if the poor things never get a wink of sleep. She's going to give Lady Hacker her money back, and she's made poor old Pa go with her in case Lady H makes a fuss."

Sam looked surprised. "I did hear something, but I thought it was the wolves in the forest. They've been howling ever such a lot lately … haven't you noticed?"

Prune shook her head. "No. Maybe it's a full moon. Doesn't that make them howl?"

"Could be." They were nearly at the bottom of the staircase, and Sam jumped the last three steps. "Aunt Egg says there aren't any wolves, but I'm sure I've seen some."

Prune snorted. "Ma doesn't WANT there to be wolves. Who would send their dear little pets to stay at Mothscale Castle if they thought there were horrible toothy wolves lurking nearby? She pretends they don't exist, and then she doesn't have to worry about them."

"AWK!" The doodlebird flapped his wings, and Sam laughed. "Dandy says she pretends *he* isn't here most of the time!"

"She'd probably like it if we weren't here either." Prune shook her head. "She likes the Royal Beasts much better than me."

"They don't argue with her," Sam pointed out. "You do, all the time."

His cousin giggled. "I do, don't I? Come on – let's find the scroll and see what we've got to do today!" She hopped across the hall, and opened the door that led to the stable yard. Sam followed close behind. His heart was beating fast ... what would the final task be? Would he be able to do it? What if everything went wrong?

The magic scroll was hidden under the hay in Prune's pony's manger.

"Darling Weebles," Prune said fondly as she pushed the hay to one side. "With any luck we'll be going out today." She found the ancient parchment, and handed it to Sam.

"Here you are, Mr Knight-in-Training. What does it say?"

Sam took the scroll, and unrolled it carefully. At first there was nothing to see, but gradually it began to feel warm ... and one by one, golden letters appeared.

"Greetings to all who wish to be Truly Noble Knights," Sam read. "For thy sixth and final task, thou must search amongst the giants who never move to discover the tower that was never built. Defeat the enemies that art not enemies, set free the captive ... and if the task is completed this very day, thou wilt at last be a Truly Noble Knight. But remember! All is not what it might seem."

"Wow!" Sam and Prune stared at each other. The doodlebird, who had been reading the scroll from his perch on a roof beam, scratched his head.

"AWK," he said. "AWK AWK AWK!"

"What's he saying?" Prune asked. "Does he know what any of that means?"

"He says he's got an idea, but he isn't sure ... he thinks we should head for the Fearsome Forest." Sam rubbed his nose. "Where's that?"

Prune grinned. "You remember the river you went swimming in when we found your sword? Well ... if you follow the river for about a mile, you'll find the Fearsome Forest. It's the dark dark forest nobody dares go into. The dark

dark forest Ma says we're never ever EVER to go near."

She slapped Sam on the back. "This'll be a REAL adventure! Let's get going!"

PINK FRILLS

It didn't take the two adventurers long to get ready. Sam fetched his sword and shield while Prune saddled Weebles, before helping Sam with Dora, his big white horse. Moments later they were riding away from the castle, heading towards the river and the Fearsome Forest.

"So," Prune asked, "do you think we're going to rescue a princess? That's what Noble Knights usually do, isn't it?" She paused, and stared thoughtfully at Weebles' ears. "H'm. What'll we do with her after we've rescued her? Ma and Pa won't exactly be thrilled if we turn up with a wishy washy princess dressed in pink frills. Or are you meant to marry her?"

Sam looked horrified. "No! Absolutely NOT! We take her back to where she belongs."

"What if she doesn't want to go? What if she falls in love with you the moment she sees you?" Prune turned round to inspect her cousin. "Although that's not exactly likely. But then again, if she hasn't seen anyone for a hundred years she won't be very fussy …"

"If she hasn't seen anyone for a hundred years she's going to be ANCIENT," Sam pointed out. "She'll want a wheelchair and a

hot water bottle, not someone to marry."

"I suppose so," Prune agreed. "And we don't actually know that it'll be a princess. The scroll just said, 'set free the captive', didn't it? It might be a canary. Or a dragon!"

"Or a prince," Sam said. "Or a queen or a witch!"

Prune snorted. "That's a stupid idea. Why would a Noble Knight rescue a witch? I reckon it'll be a princess."

Sam, knowing Prune would never let him have the last word, decided not to answer, and they rode on in silence.

The river was much wilder than Sam had expected. It roared between the rocky banks, twirling huge broken branches round and round as if they were tiny twigs. On the far side tall trees loomed darkly, and a chill ran down Sam's spine.

"Ummm ..." he said. "Erm ... how do we get across?"

Prune gave him a despising stare. "There's a bridge, of course."

"Oh." Sam patted Dora for comfort. Prune stood up in her stirrups to peer ahead, and let out a whoop of triumph.

"There's the bridge! Come on, Sam! I'll race you! Last one there's a numpty!" And she set off at a gallop.

Sam, taken by surprise, didn't stand a chance. He and Dora arrived to find Prune already on the other side of the rickety old bridge, waiting for him with a smug smile. "Weebles is the best! Always beats the rest!"

"You didn't give me a fair start," Sam said crossly as he and Dora carefully made their way across. The wooden planks were old and rotten, and in places had fallen away completely. Dora took her time, testing each step, and Sam was more than happy to let her.

"Phew," he said as they reached solid ground. "Doesn't look as if anyone's been over that for centuries!"

"Don't expect they have," Prune agreed. "The villagers never come here. There are loads of stories about horrible monsters – hopefully we'll meet some!"

"Yes," Sam said, and he sat up straighter. "And rescue the princess!"

As they left the bridge and drew nearer, the trees at the edge of the Fearsome Forest seemed to grow taller and darker. The doodlebird, who had been flying above them, flew down and perched on Sam's shoulder.

"Awk," he remarked.

Sam pulled Dora to a sudden halt. "Wolves?" he asked. "You can see wolves? REAL wolves?"

"He's not going to see unreal wolves, silly," Prune said. "But that's exciting! Are they big and fierce with sharp teeth and drooling jaws?"

The doodlebird put his head on one side. "Awk Awk Awk."

"Oh." Sam sounded relieved, and Prune looked at him suspiciously.

"Aren't they wolves after all?"

"It's an old grandmother wolf and three little ones," Sam translated. "Dandy says they look friendly ... he says the little ones waved at him."

Prune frowned. "That doesn't sound right. Is he sure they weren't trying to catch him for their dinner?"

"AWK." The doodlebird fluffed up his feathers, and looked indignant. "AWK!"

"OK," Prune said. "Even I understood that. So what are we waiting for? Let's go and meet these friendly wolves. Maybe they can tell us where to find the giants who never move." She shook her reins, and Weebles broke into a trot. Sam and Dora followed, and soon they were weaving their way between towering tree trunks.

"Woooooooooooooooowl!"

Weebles swerved into a prickly bramble
bush, and Dora stopped so suddenly that Sam
fell forward on her neck. "Ooooof," he said as
he pulled himself back into his saddle.

"Ouch!" Prune picked a large thorn out of
her knee and stared round. "Was that a wolf?
Where is it?"

"Grrirrrrrrr … here," said a growly
voice, and an elderly wolf
stepped out from behind
a tree. "Welcome
to Fearsome
Forest, my
dears. Cubs?
Come and
say hello
to our
visitors!"

"Shan't shan't shan't!" Three small wolf cubs tumbled into view, and stuck out their tongues at Sam and Prune. "Nasty nasty NASTY humans!"

The grandmother wolf shook her head. "Now now, my darlings. Not all humans are nasty, you know … and these are human cubs, not grown-ups."

The biggest wolf cub was staring at Sam. "Why you got a sword, human? Goin' to chop our tailsies off? Just you try! I'll bite bite BITE you!" And he showed his sharp little teeth.

Sam did his best to bow. "I'm Sam J. Butterbiggins, and I'm a knight-in-training. And it's sort of traditional to have a sword and a shield if you're a knight. And I wouldn't dream of hurting you."

The other two wolf cubs nudged each other, and sniggered loudly. "Oooooh! 'He wouldn't

dream of hurting us!' Aren't we lucky lucky
little wolfies? Snapper's scared him good and
proper! Hee hee hee! Let's give the big brave
knight a cheer!" And they fell on the forest
floor in a fit of giggles, blocking the path.

"Aren't they the sweetest little poppets?"
The grandmother wolf looked delighted, but
Prune was not impressed.

"No. They're being rude. Sam's here on an
important quest. If you'll just tell them to move
we'll get on our way."

"Oh, hoity toity!" The grandmother wolf
shook her head at Prune, and the cubs stayed

where they were. "An important quest, indeed. And what might that be, then?"

The three little cubs rolled their eyes. "What's big brave Sammy looking for? A wiggly wiggly worm, or a scary hairy ghostie? Hee hee hee hee hee!"

Sam was feeling uncomfortable. He knew Prune was getting cross, and he was worried in case she lost her temper. He glanced from side to side to see if they could  ride round the wolf cub family – and saw with a start that they were being watched. Another wolf was leaning casually against a birch tree, and as Sam looked at him he raised a shaggy eyebrow.

"Word of warning," he said quietly. "Be nice to those cubs. Their dad's a big cheese in this forest, and he's a doting father. Upset him, and you'll never be seen again. He has … what shall I call them? Helpers. He calls them his Cuddlies, but cuddly they're not. You really really REALLY don't want to get into their clutches …"

"Oh!" Sam's stomach looped a loop. He glanced at Prune, who was scowling heavily, and hurriedly swung himself off Dora's back. The three little wolf cubs stopped giggling and stared at him.

"What d'you want, Sammy diddums?" Snapper demanded, and he danced in a circle under Sam's nose. "My name's Snapper! I'm so clever ... I'm the cleverest wolf cub ever!"

Sam took a deep breath.

"Wow! The cleverest wolf cub ever? You're just

what we've been looking for! Someone very clever who can help us!"

Snapper stopped dancing, and gave Sam a suspicious look. "You telling fibs?"

"No." Sam crossed his fingers behind his back and did his best to sound as if he meant every word. "We need to find the giants that never move, and—"

"Sam!" Prune glared at him. "We don't need any silly little—"

"Ideas from me." Sam nodded enthusiastically, hoping Prune would guess he had a reason for interrupting. "You're quite right, Lady Prunella. Absolutely right. I have VERY silly ideas!"

Prune looked at Sam in astonishment. "WHAT?"

"So," Sam went on before she could say anything else, "what ideas do YOU have,

Snapper?"

Snapper scratched his ear, and frowned as if he was thinking hard. "Giants? Big ones?"

"And they never move," Sam said encouragingly.

The wolf cub scratched his other ear. "Never moving. Like trees?"

For a moment there was a stunned silence, and then Sam punched the air.

"Woooooooooooo!" he gave a yell of triumph. "You really are the cleverest wolf cub ever! Of COURSE ... the giants who never move are trees! That's why Dandy said we should come to the Fearsome Forest!"

"AWK." The doodlebird nodded, and hopped onto a lower branch.

Snapper blinked. "Giants? Oh … OH!" As he gradually realised what he had said, he looked more and more pleased with himself. "Oh yes. That's me. Cleverest wolf cub ever!"

"Thank you very much," Sam said. "And now maybe you could help us find – what was it, Prune?"

"A tower that was never built," Prune said. She leant down from her pony, and hissed in Sam's ear, "Sam! Stop it!

We don't want any help from a silly little wolf cub. He's SO annoying—"

"Sssssh," Sam warned, but Snapper had heard her.

"And YOU'RE a nasty girly whirly weaselly wiffly wump!" He put his paw on Sam's arm. "He's my friend! And we're going exploring!" He turned to his brothers. "Go home with Gran. I'm busy!"

Sam looked at the grandmother wolf, expecting her to take no notice of this instruction, but she nodded. "Such a clever little wolfie! Just like his daddy! Gives his orders, and off we go!"

"But we want to go tooooooo," the brothers wailed.

"Another time, my little darlings," the grandmother told them.

As they disappeared into the

darkness of the forest, Prune pounced on Sam. "Sam! Why are you being so nice to that stupid wolf cub? He'll only get in the way. We can find the tower ourselves ... I'm sure we can!"

"Weaselly wiffly wump – be quiet!" Snapper bared his teeth. "I'm not stupid! You're not to call me names! I'm going to tell my daddy on you! Gibble? Gibble! Where are you?"

The wolf with the shaggy eyebrows came out from the shadows, shrugging as he walked past Sam. "I did try to warn you."

Prune stared. "Who are you?"

"Gibble's the name. Nursemaid, dogsbody, general help – that's me. Meant to keep an eye on the cubs." The wolf shrugged again. "It's a job."

"Gibble! Tell my daddy I need the Cuddlies!" Snapper stamped all four of his feet.

The wolf hesitated. "The Cuddlies? Are you sure?"

"Do as I say, Gibble!" The wolf cub's voice was shrill. "I don't want to be called nasty names! Tell my daddy! Tell him NOW!"

Gibble bowed. "Just as you say, Master

Snapper." He threw back his head, and a long howl echoed across the forest. For a moment there was silence, and then came an answering howl.

"The Cuddlies'll teach you to be nice!" Snapper glared at Prune.

Prune glared back. "I'll be nice to you when you're nice to me," she said. "And you shouldn't go running to your daddy if someone upsets you. You have to stand up for yourself. I do."

Sam, remembering Prune's clashes with her mother, shuddered. *Sometimes,* he thought, *life is easier if you try a little friendliness and tact.* With this in mind, he smiled his most soothing smile.

"Why don't we start looking for the tower?" he suggested. "Snapper, you're welcome to come – but Prune's my True Companion, and I can't finish my tasks without her. And if I don't finish my sixth task today, I'll never be a Very Noble Knight!" The idea that he might not complete his sixth task made a lump rise in Sam's throat. He took a deep breath and went on, "And that's what I want more than anything else in the whole wide world."

Snapper looked puzzled. "Very Noble Knight? What does they do?"

Sam's eyes shone. "They do good deeds! They go on quests to rescue people in trouble, or to find precious things that are lost. They stay loyal to their friends. They choose good over evil, and help the poor and needy. They're ... they're just the BEST!"

"Is there Very Noble Wolves?" Snapper sounded thoughtful, and Sam looked at him in surprise. "I don't see why not."

"Huh!" Prune snorted loudly. "Very Noble Wolves wouldn't get their daddy to sort their problems. They'd do it themselves."

The wolf cub stuck out his tongue. "And a Very Noble Wiffly Wump would be nice to wolf cubs!"

Prune went purple. For a moment Sam wondered if she was about to explode – but instead she began to laugh. "Fair enough. Friends?" And she jumped off her pony and held out her hand.

Snapper hesitated. "Will you help Snapper be a Very Noble Wolf?"

"We'll try," Sam said, and the wolf cub gave him his paw.

"Friends," said Snapper. He gave Prune a sideways look. "Maybe we be friends later."

"OK," Prune said. "Now – can we get on
with finding the tower that was never built?"
She climbed back on to Weebles, and picked
up her reins. "Snapper … you can go first.
Let's head for the middle of the forest!"

"Hang on a minute!" It was Gibble.
"Haven't you forgotten something? What
about the Cuddlies? They'll be on their way …
and you should get out of here! Both of you!
Get out while you can!"

"Bother the Cuddlies," Prune said
cheerfully. "We don't care about them, do we,
Sam?"

Sam was back on Dora, and he smiled at
Gibble. "No! We're all friends now."

Gibble shook his head. "If
only it was that easy. Oh well.
Don't say I didn't warn you …"

DINNER FOR THE CUDDLIES

The deeper they rode into the forest, the more Sam thought that *giants* was the perfect description for the trees. Many of them had faces, and a tall oak winked at him as he guided Dora past.

"Do the trees here move about?" he asked.

Snapper was too far ahead to hear the question, but Gibble, who was loping along beside him, shook his head.

"Too heavy," he said. "The young ones walk about a bit, but the older ones don't. Their roots go too far down."

A birch tree leant over, tweaked Sam's hair, and straightened itself with a chuckle as he gave a protesting "OUCH!"

"They're suspicious of humans," Gibble explained. "You should be safe enough, though. It isn't as if you were carrying an axe. Well ... you'll be safe from the trees, anyway."

Sam rubbed his nose. "What do you mean? We won't be bothered by anything else, will we?"

Gibble looked uncomfortable. "Surely you haven't forgotten! I sent out a call for the Cuddlies ..."

"But there's no problem." Sam pointed to Prune and Snapper, who were chatting happily. "They're getting on really well—"

"AAAAAAAAAAAAA AAAAAAAAAAGH!"

It was Prune's voice …
but Prune had vanished.
Weebles was standing under
a low branch looking
puzzled, and Snapper
was staring at the
riderless pony with
his mouth wide
open.
**"HELP!
SAM!"**

The cry came from high up in the branches.

Sam squinted up through the rustling leaves, and caught a brief glimpse of his cousin being tossed from one tree to another by the most hideous creatures he had ever seen. One had three eyes and tentacles, and was trailing slime. The other – and it had more arms than Sam could count – was juggling Prune as if she were a beach ball.

"What are THOSE?" He rubbed his eyes and looked again – but Prune had gone.

Gibble sighed. "Those, my friend, are the Cuddlies."

"But ..." Sam was pale and trembling. "What will they do with her?"

"Nobody knows. Nobody's ever dared to go to their lair." Gibble coughed. "Ahem. I'm afraid she may have gone for good."

Sam stared at him, then frowned. "No she hasn't," he said. "I'm Sam J. Butterbiggins, knight-in-training, and nobody takes my True Companion prisoner! I'm going to find her, and bring her back!" He looked round for the doodlebird. "Dandy? Where are you?"

There was no answer. For a moment Sam's heart sank; had Dandy been captured too? But Snapper came running back along the path bursting with news.

"The bird followed them!" he said. "I seed

him! He flew after the Cuddlies!" Seeing Sam's face, he came to a sudden halt. "Oooooh … are you cross with Snapper? Cos it was me called the Cuddlies?" He hung his head, and began to whimper.

Sam was struggling with his feelings. The wolf cub was right … but then again, perhaps it was just as much his fault. After all, Gibble had told him to be careful, and he hadn't warned Prune.

A thought came to him, and he looked hopefully at Snapper. "Couldn't you ask your dad to make them bring her back?"

Snapper began to whimper even louder, and Gibble shook his head. "We've been told they always keep what they capture." He paused. "For ever."

"Well – this time they won't." Sam folded his arms. "I'm not leaving here until I've found

Prune. As soon as Dandy
tells me which way to
go, I'm off."

"Me too." Snapper
jumped to his feet. "I'll
help!"

Gibble held up a warning paw. "Your
dad wouldn't like that, Master Snapper!"

"Don't care." Snapper gave a low growl.
"Snapper's going too!" He peered up at Sam.
"What do you say, knight-in-training?"

Sam was staring into the sky, waiting for the
doodlebird to come back. "What? Oh, that's
OK. If Gibble doesn't mind."

"It's my job," Gibble said wearily. "Where
he goes, I go. Orders. Lose him, and I'll
be joining the young lady as the Cuddlies'
dinner—"

"DINNER?" Sam swung round. "You didn't

say anything about dinner!"

"Nobody's ever told me what they do,"
Gibble said. "But they have a very big stew
pot."

Sam shuddered. He had only had a brief
glimpse of the Cuddlies, but it had been
enough. "We need to find Prune really really
quickly," he said, and he rode forward to catch
hold of Weebles' reins.
The pony, however,
had other ideas.
He was listening,
his ears twitching,
and as Sam came
closer he threw
up his
head and
neighed.
A moment

57

later he was cantering away between the trees.
Dora whinnied a reply, and trotted after him.

"You've got to go faster, Dora," Sam urged.
"Gallop! We've got to catch Weebles! If he

goes back to the
castle without Prune,
Aunt Egg will have
hysterics—"

"AWK!" The doodlebird appeared in a
flurry of feathers, and Dora slowed again.
"AWK AWK AWK!"

"Really? We should follow Weebles?" Sam
looked at Dandy in surprise. "Isn't he going
home?"

The doodlebird shook his head. "AWK."

Snapper was watching Sam with eyes like
saucers. "Can you really understand that bird?"

"Of course," Sam said. "He says Weebles can
hear Prune yelling, and he's off to fetch her, so
we should follow him. Dandy says it isn't far –
he watched the Cuddlies all the way back to a
little clearing."

"I can't hear anything." Snapper scratched

his ears. "Can you hear anything, Gibble?"

Gibble shook his head. "Too old and too deaf."

"Prune always says Weebles can hear her ninety miles away," Sam told them. "She must be right."

"AWK," agreed the doodlebird, and then, "AWK AWK!"

Sam stared at him in horror. "You saw the Cuddlies lighting a fire? Oh NO! I've got to save her ... we can hunt for the princess afterwards. Come on, Dora!"

GRUMPY
BRAMBLES

It was a strange-looking rescue party. The doodlebird flew above the riderless Weebles, who was followed by Sam on Dora. Both animals were going as fast as they dared through the thick forest undergrowth, and behind them ran a panting wolf cub and a whiskery wolf.

In and out of the trees they went; some of the little birches drew back to let them through, but the older oaks and beeches grunted disapproval and stayed where they were.

"I'm too old for this," Gibble complained as they came hurrying out into a small grassy hollow where Weebles was standing, flicking his ears as if he were listening. "Master Snapper – don't you think you ought to go home?"

Snapper shook his head. "Don't want to! YOU go home!"

Gibble sighed. "I wish I could."

Sam waved up at the doodlebird. "Are we nearly there?"

"AWK." The doodlebird flapped a wing

towards a small gap between
two large pine trees.

"Oh ..." Sam slid off Dora's back. "I should
go on foot?"

The doodlebird nodded, and Weebles gave
a short sharp whinny of agreement. He gave
Sam a meaningful look, then began to graze.
Dora, delighted, went to join him.

Snapper bounced up to Sam. "Is we ready?"

"Ready," Sam said. He gripped his shield,
and made sure his sword was loose in its
scabbard. "Here goes!" And he tiptoed towards
the pine trees, Snapper at his heels and an
unwilling Gibble loping after
them.

The path on the other side of the trees twisted this way and that until Sam had no idea which way to go. If the doodlebird hadn't been flying above him, he would have been completely lost.

"Dandy! I thought you said it was quite near," he panted as he paused for breath. A particularly grumpy bramble had torn his tunic while trying to remove his sword, and he was beginning to wonder if he was ever going to find Prune.

"AWK AWK AWK!" the doodlebird said encouragingly.

"It's all very well for you," Sam complained. "You can fly! But I feel as if I'm just going round in circles."

"AWK!"

"That's exactly what we're doing." Gibble forced his way through the bramble bush, puffing and panting. "The Cuddlies don't want to be found – and they don't need a path. They swing from tree to tree."

Sam shuddered at the memory. "Yes."

"So you're going in a spiral," Gibble explained. "Round and round ... and it'll get worse."

"No!" Sam stood up straight. "A knight-in-training is not defeated by a few bushes. I'm going on!"

"Me too," said Snapper.

Gibble heaved a heavy sigh. "You should be going home, Master Snapper."

"NO!" Snapper scowled at the old wolf. "You stay here if you're tired."

"But—" Gibble began.

"No no NO! I'll tell Dad I ordered you! Stay here!" The wolf cub held up a paw.

"I'll do my best to look after him," Sam promised, and Gibble shook his head.

"Mind you do … or you'll have the Cuddlies after you. My old legs are worn out …" and he curled up in a clump of bracken. A moment later Sam heard him beginning to snore.

The next part of the journey was hardest of all. Sam had to scramble through sharp thorn bushes and squeeze between jagged rocks, then balance his way across several wobbly tree trunks laid across a green and quivering bog. Snapper wailed pathetically when he saw the bog, and Sam was forced to carry him. His arms were aching by the time he reached the path again.

"You weigh a ton, Snapper," he said as he put him down on the ground.

"Sniff! Smoke!" Snapper's nose quivered, and Sam paused.

The wolf cub was right. There was a definite smell of wood smoke,  and as Sam moved cautiously onwards he could hear the faint crackle of burning sticks. A few steps more and he could see a small clearing ahead.

"AWK..." the doodlebird said. "AWK..."

Gradually the smoke grew thicker, and Sam had to swallow hard to stop himself from coughing. Looking round he saw a tall pine tree with branches low enough to climb; he put his finger to his lips and bent down to whisper in Snapper's ear. "I'm going to climb to the top to see if I can see Prune," he breathed.

Snapper nodded and sat down, and Sam began to climb. He was a little more than half way up when a gust of wind blew the smoke away, and he had a clear view ... and his eyes widened.

There was indeed a fire – and the two Cuddlies were throwing branches on to the blazing pile to make it burn higher and higher. There was no sign of Prune, but Sam turned cold when he saw the huge cauldron propped against the trunk of an enormous hollow oak tree. Beside the cauldron were heaps of neatly sliced carrots, onions and cabbages – and a large ladle.

Oh no! Sam thought. *They're getting ready to cook something ...*

Very carefully, holding his breath and
moving one inch at a time, he edged his way
along a branch until he was near enough to
hear what the Cuddlies were saying. At first
they were too busy, but then one dropped a log
on his tentacles and let out such a shrill screech
that Sam all but lost his balance.

"Oogly moogly, Bobbly Bob," said the larger Cuddly. "What's the matter, ugly mugly? Is nearly time to gobble gobble gobble!"

"Hurt my tiddly tentacles," Bob said. "Hurt BADLY, Geoff!"

Geoff snorted. "Serves you rightly tightly, Bobbly Bob. Be more careful!"

Bob's green cheeks were wet with tears. "Poor Bobbly Bob! Poor Bobbly!"

There was another snort, and Geoff stomped his way towards the cauldron. "Time to put potty pot on the fire, Bob! Time for cooky wooky gobble gobble time!" He rubbed his oversized stomach. "Yummy yummy gobble gobble! Geoff is happy! Let's get gobble grub ready!"

Sam held his breath. Were they going to bring Prune out from some hiding place? Or – and his heart began to beat faster – could she be in the cauldron already? He crept a little further along the branch so he could peer inside, but saw nothing but greenish yellowish slime.

"Phew," he murmured. "That looks revolting!"

He was about to make his way back to the safety of the pine's solid trunk when a flutter of wings caught his eye.

The doodlebird was perched on the top of the hollow oak tree, peering in. Inching his way a little further so he could see what was  interesting the bird so much, Sam saw he was looking down at a handkerchief tied to the end of a stick ...

and a wonderfully familiar face. "Get me out of here!" it mouthed, "and hurry up about it!"

Sam beamed. "Prune! It's you!"

In his excitement he had spoken out loud. At once both Geoff and Bob froze.

"What that, Bobbly Bob?" Geoff whispered.

"Creepy weepy spy!" Bob's three eyes were staring in three different directions. Geoff put his scaly snout in the air and sniffed loudly.

"Can maybe smell wolfie," he said. "Why

wolfies come here?"

Sam, clinging to his branch, glanced down. Snapper was sitting bolt upright, and his ears were twitching.

"Bobbly Bob look round," Bob said, and he scuttled round the fire at surprising speed.

"Lookie look," Geoff agreed, and he thundered towards Sam's tree.

Something had to be done.

Sam grabbed a couple of pine cones and threw them as hard as he could to the other side of the clearing, where they landed in a pile of leaves with a satisfactory rustling noise.

At once the Cuddlies stopped their rush, and hurtled in the opposite direction. Sam took the opportunity to slide down his tree, almost landing on top of Snapper.

"Prune's inside the oak tree!" he whispered. "I've got to get her out!" He looked wildly round, but there were no useful vines or anything that could be twisted into a rope. "A ladder!" Sam's brain was whirling. "What could I use for a ladder?"

Snapper scratched his ear. "Don't know."

Bob and Geoff were searching in the leaves,

muttering to each other. Seeing that they were about to move away, Sam scooped up a stone and threw it into the middle of a bramble bush. The Cuddlies paused. Then, with a speed that amazed Sam, they ran up the trunk of a nearby tree so they could peer into the brambles from above.

Sam was getting desperate. "I can't keep throwing things. Snapper – do you really REALLY want to be a Very Noble Wolf? Could you keep them busy, while I try and climb the pine tree again? If I can get a branch to bend down far enough, I might just be able to pull Prune out …"

Snapper looked thrilled. "I'm the cleverest wolf cub ever!" he said. Sliding between the trees he began his task of distracting the Cuddlies by whistling loudly, then creeping away to rustle in a pile of leaves.

Sam scrambled up the pine tree
for the second time. "This might
just work," he told himself as he
crawled his way along a long branch
that hung over the oak tree. As he got closer
and closer the branch began to bend, and he
tried hard not to imagine what would happen
if it broke.

"Think positive!" he murmured, and at that
moment he saw Prune below him. She had
managed to heap up the broken wood inside
the hollow trunk, and had climbed up as far as
she could. Sam, hanging on to the branch with
one arm, held out the other.

He was too high.

With a wriggle and a squirm, he moved
further down the branch … and he could
reach. He grabbed Prune's outstretched hand,
and the branch gave an ominous creak.

"Oh no!" Sam shut his eyes, and held on
… and at the same time began to try to move
backwards. The branch creaked again, more
loudly.

"Swing me!"
Prune demanded.
"Swing me as high
as you can!"
Sam gritted his
teeth, and began to
swing her to and fro.
"HIGHER!" Prune hissed.
The branch swayed wildly – and she let
go. Sam opened his eyes, and saw her pulling

herself along a lower branch with the ease of a monkey. A moment later she was safely on the ground, waiting for him.

For a long moment Sam was too exhausted to move. Then, with a huge effort, he made himself crawl back to join her.

"Hi," he said, and waited for her to thank him. Far from being grateful, however, Prune was scowling.

"You've been AGES!" she said. "I thought I was going to be turned into Prune stew!"

"Wooooooooooo!" Snapper's plaintive howl echoed across the clearing. "Wooooooo! Put me dooooooown!"

Sam and Prune swung round – and saw Geoff stomping towards them, Snapper held tightly in his arms.

Bob was close behind … and they were both smiling wide toothy smiles.

"Gotcher," said Geoff.

"Gobble Bobble," Bob agreed.

BYE BYE,
BAD PEOPLE

Sam and Prune stood still, frozen to the spot.

"Woooooooo!" Snapper was wriggling
and squirming in Geoff's arms. "Don't
want to be nobbly wolfie any more ...
let me gooooooooo!"

Sam swallowed hard.
This was his moment ... the
moment when a knight-in-
training could show his true
self.

"Defeat the enemies!"
he muttered. "Defeat the
enemies!" He pulled his
sword out of its scabbard,
and waved it in the air.

"Hideous monsters!" he said. "I, Sam
J. Butterbiggins, am here to rescue your
prisoners! Let the wolfcub go!!!!!" And he ran
at Geoff.

"Go, Sam, GO!" Prune yelled. "Biff them!
Boff them! Bash them—"

Geoff shrieked and dropped Snapper, and
Snapper dashed for the safety of the forest …
and as he went he tripped up Bob, and Bob
crashed into Geoff –

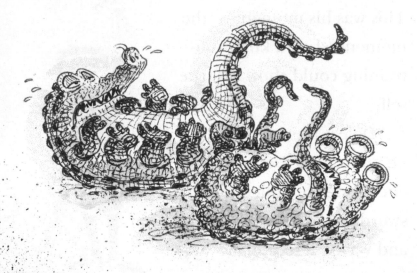

and they both burst into floods of tears and
rolled on the ground with their legs in the air.

"He wants to hurt poor
Bobbly Bob," Bob wailed.
"He called us hideous
monsters!" sobbed Geoff.
"Just wanted to give
him little wolfie," Bob
hiccupped.

"To give him little wolfie," Geoff echoed,
and they began crying louder than ever.

Sam stared at them. "But you were going to
put Prune in a stew!"

The Cuddlies stopped crying as suddenly as
if Sam had turned off a switch.

"STEW?" they said together.

"Yes!" Sam folded his arms, and Prune did
the same. "You were lighting your fire—"

"AND putting your cauldron on to boil."

Prune nodded her agreement. "And I heard you! After you dropped me in that horrible tree trunk you kept talking about gobble gobble gobbling!"

Bob blinked his three bulging eyes, and his mouth opened wider and wider in astonishment. "But we gobble gobbles cabbages! And onions! And carrotty carrots!" He rolled himself back onto his little legs. "We NEVER gobbles meaty bone things! Yuck yuck YUCK!"

Geoff struggled back onto his feet, and wiped his nose on his tail. "Yuck yuck YUCKETTY YUCK!"

Sam shook his head. "You mean ... you

mean you don't eat the people you catch? So
what DO you do with them? Gibble said they're
never seen again!"

The Cuddlies looked at each other, and said
nothing. Then Bob waved a tentacle. "Does we
tell, Geoff?"

Geoff shifted anxiously from foot to foot.
"Don't know, Bobbly Bob. Can't think!" He
pointed at Sam's sword. "Nasty sharp pointy
thing! Makes my poorly head go jittery!"

Sam put his sword back in its scabbard.
"There you are. Now, tell us!"

The two Cuddlies looked at each other again, and Geoff sidled closer. "Is a secret! If chief Wolfie knew, us wouldn't be scary no more …"

Bob shivered. "Would tell Cuddlies no more cabbage. No more carrotty carrots. No more onions if not making Nasty Meaty People Stew!"

Sam threw back his shoulders. "You have the word of Sam J. Butterbiggins, knight-in-training. Your secret will be safe with me."

Prune straightened her tunic. "And you have the word of Prune, True Companion to Sam J. Butterbiggins."

Bob was almost standing on

Sam's feet in his terror of being overheard. "Come come see …" he whispered, and he beckoned with a tentacle before scuttling away towards the oak where Prune had been kept prisoner.

Prune nudged Sam. "Is this a trick?"

Sam didn't answer. Something was niggling in his memory. "I'm trying to remember what the scroll said … didn't it say something about defeating enemies who were friends?"

"It might have done." Prune still sounded suspicious, but as they walked past the oak tree she gave a gasp. "OH! Sam! Look! Could this be the tower that was never built? It was never built, because it grew!"

Sam felt a flutter of excitement that quickly died. The tree did look like a tower ... but there had been no sign of any princess. He sighed, and tried to ignore the feeling of disappointment that was making his stomach feel as if it was full of cold stones.

Bob and Geoff were leading the way to a well-worn path. On either side were piles of carefully stacked  empty barrels; Sam looked at them in surprise, but Bob and Geoff offered no explanation.

"Sh!" Prune stopped, and held up a finger. "Can you hear water?"

"AWK!" The doodlebird agreed.

"Yes ..." Sam nodded, and even as he spoke they came out from the shade of the trees and he saw the river. It was narrower than it had been when they crossed the bridge into the forest, but it was flowing just as fast, if not faster.

"There!" The Cuddlies pointed to the river. "There is bye bye bad people!"

"What?" Sam peered anxiously at the rippling water. "You don't mean you push them in and let them drown, do you?"

Geoff looked offended. "We isn't NASTY Cuddlies! We is SCARY ... not NASTY."

"So what's the secret?" Prune asked.

Bob chuckled. "Easy peasy. Drop bad people in hollow tree ..."

"Give a little drinkie drink of slimy slime ..." Geoff began to jump up and down.

"People sleepy sleepy sleep sleep!" Bob spun in a circle. "Carry sleepy people out of hollow tree ..."

"Pop in a barrel …" Geoff's eyes were shining.

"And off they goes! Down the river, away away away!" The Cuddlies gave each other a high five, and beamed at Prune and Sam.

"Goodness!" Sam said. "That's … erm … really clever! Don't you think so, Prune?"

Prune was looking thoughtful. "Yes," she said. "And do you know what, Sam? We can get home in double quick time if we go the same way!"

"WHAT?" The knight-in-training stared at his True Companion. "You mean … us go in a barrel?"

"It'll be fun," Prune told him. "Come on! We'll never get back in time for tea if we have to go all the way back through the forest. Look how low the sun is … Ma'll be FURIOUS if she gets back before we do!"

"But what about Dora and Weebles?" Sam asked.

"I'll call for Weebles. He'll hear me. He always does."

"AWK," the doodlebird said, "AWK!"

Prune laughed. "There you are. Dandy'll tell Dora! They can meet us at the bridge." She turned to Bob and Geoff. "Can we borrow a barrel?"

The Cuddlies nodded. "Yes yes yes!" and Geoff stomped off to fetch one.

Bob waved his tentacles. "Goodie goodie good! See if barrel floats!"

Sam spun round to stare at him. "Don't you know if they float?"

"Oooooh …" The tentacles drooped. Bob

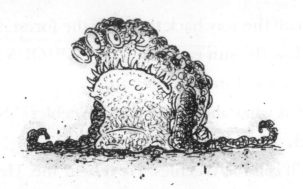

went a curious shade of purple, and Sam
guessed he was blushing.

"What's the matter?" he asked.

The Cuddly crept towards him. "Never
have caught bad person," he whispered.
"Not yet!"

Geoff, pulling a large barrel behind him,
heard what Bob was saying. "But we is ready
steady ready! Hey, Bobbly Bob?"

Bob nodded. "Is all ready. Drop in tree …"

"Drink sleepy slime …" Geoff sang.

"Sleepy sleepy sleep sleep …"

"Pop in barrel …"

"Off they goes!"

"And here's big big
barrel!" Geoff dropped the
barrel in the river with a splash.

Prune grabbed Sam's arm. "Come on, Sam!
Let's sail off home!"

SILVER AND GOLD

Much to Sam's relief the barrel did float. It also turned round and round and round, and if he hadn't already been feeling sick with disappointment he would have felt sick from the endless spinning. On and on it spun, and Sam shut his eyes tightly ...

Prune was enjoying herself enormously. She waved an enthusiastic goodbye to the Cuddlies, and Sam was convinced she was about to upset the barrel.

"Sit down, Prune!" he wailed. "Sit down!"

"But I can see Snapper and Gibble!" Prune began to wave even more wildly. "Gibble! GIBBLE! Snapper saved us! He's a hero! He deserves a medal! Sam – you've got to say thank you to Snapper!"

"Thank you, Snapper ..." Sam's face was green, and he was hanging on to the barrel's sides. "Prune! I'm going to be sick!"

"You can't be," Prune told him. "Look! There's the bridge! And hurrah! Weebles and Dora and the doodlebird are there! Get ready to grab something, or we'll end up miles away ..."

Sam gulped, and stretched out an arm, but the barrel had ideas of its own. With a final spin it crashed into the wooden supports, bounced away to the muddy bank, and came to a rocking halt. Prune and Sam scrambled out, and the barrel sank.

"WHOOOOOOO!" Prune punched the air. "Wasn't that AMAZING?"

"No," Sam said. "It wasn't." He walked slowly over to his big white horse, and leant his head against her side.

Prune stared at him. "What's the matter?"

"What's the matter?" Sam swung round. "What's the MATTER? I failed the last task, didn't I? I never rescued a princess! I'll never be a Very Noble Knight now … not ever."

"SAM!" Prune looked at him as if he had gone completely mad. "I knew you were stupid, but I never thought you were this stupid! Don't you see? You did EXACTLY what the scroll said!"

"No I didn't—" Sam began, but Prune interrupted.

"You found the giants," she said. "Didn't you?"

Sam nodded. "I suppose so ..."

"You did. And you found the tower."

Sam looked doubtful. "If you were right about the hollow tree ..."

"I was. I always am. And you defeated the enemies who turned out to be friendly, AND you rescued a captive!"

"It was only a wolf cub," Sam said gloomily, "and he wasn't even a captive. They were bringing him back to us—"

Prune, about to explode, took him by the shoulders and shook him. "But SAM! Who did you rescue from the tree?"

"Well, you, I suppose," Sam said, "but ..."

There was a long silence.

"Oh." Sam went pink. "Oh! I DID rescue someone! I rescued YOU!" He blushed even deeper. "The scroll said 'all is not what it might seem', didn't it? I forgot."

Prune heaved an enormous sigh. "What have I just been telling you? And ... and Sam! Look at yourself!"

Sam looked down ... and let out a long whistle of astonishment. His tunic was shining silver, and his belt was gleaming gold.

He glanced at Prune, and saw she had a scarlet sash over her shoulder with a large golden badge.

"You're not a knight-in-training any more, Sam," she said. "You're a Knight! And I'm a REAL True Companion!"

Sam was speechless.

He pinched himself hard, and it hurt … and then he saw Dora. Her bridle was red and silver, and a silver helmet hung from the scarlet leather saddle.

"Of course," Prune went on, "I don't know if you're Very Noble yet … but I reckon you'll do. Come on. Let's get home."

"But what'll Aunt Egg say when she sees us?" Sam asked. "Your mother hates knights, and everything like that!"

"That's why we need to get back before she does," Prune told him. "Now, HURRY!"

Sam nodded, and picked up the helmet. Hardly daring to believe what he was doing, he put it on and turned to Prune. "Does it look OK?"

Prune snorted. "You look like a pepper pot," she said, and then she paused. "Well – sort of. Actually ..." she paused again. "It kind of suits you. Come on. Let's GO!"

So that's it! I've done it! I'm a Very Noble Knight ... although I'm not quite ready to tell Aunt Egg about it. But I know, and Prune — the best True Companion in the whole wide world (I won't tell her that. She's quite big-headed enough already) — knows, and that's enough for me.

Next? We'll go adventuring! Sam J. Butterbiggins, Very Noble Knight, and his True Companion, the Lady Prunella of Mothscale Castle!
 HURRAH!!!!

P.S. I've just read that last bit
to Dandy. All he said was, "AWK!"
I think that means,

"THE END!"

GOBLINS

Beware - there are goblins living among us!

Within these pages lies a glimpse into their secret world. But read quickly, and speak softly, in case the goblins spot you...

A riotous, laugh-out-loud funny series for younger readers from the bestselling author of **HUGLESS DOUGLAS**, David Melling.